DATE DUE

JAN 0 8 1996		
JUN 9 1998		
JUL 6 1998		
SEP 19 '05		

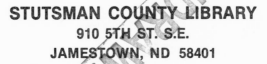

STUTSMAN COUNTY LIBRARY
BOOKMOBILE
Books for Everyone

OEMCO

A NOTE TO PARENTS

When your children are ready to "step into reading," giving them the right books—and lots of them—is as crucial as giving them the right food to eat. **Step into Reading Books** present exciting stories and information reinforced with lively, colorful illustrations that make learning to read fun, satisfying, and worthwhile. They are priced so that acquiring an entire library of them is affordable. And they are beginning readers with an important difference—they're written on four levels.

Step 1 Books, with their very large type and extremely simple vocabulary, have been created for the very youngest readers. **Step 2 Books** are both longer and slightly more difficult. **Step 3 Books,** written to mid-second-grade reading levels, are for the child who has acquired even greater reading skills. **Step 4 Books** offer exciting nonfiction for the increasingly proficient reader.

Children develop at different ages. **Step into Reading Books,** with their four levels of reading, are designed to help children become good—and interested—readers *faster*. The grade levels assigned to the four steps—preschool through grade 1 for Step 1, grades 1 through 3 for Step 2, grades 2 and 3 for Step 3, and grades 2 through 4 for Step 4—are intended only as guides. Some children move through all four steps very rapidly; others climb the steps over a period of several years. These books will help your child "step into reading" in style!

To my
uncle Leon
(old ham),
one of
the best
—P. McK.

To Peter
—P. M.

Step into Reading

Monkey-Monkey's Trick

Based on an African Folk Tale

By Patricia McKissack
Illustrated by Paul Meisel

A Step 2 Book

Random House ⌂ New York

Library of Congress Cataloging-in-Publication Data:
McKissack, Pat, 1944- Monkey-Monkey's trick. (Step into reading. A Step 2 book) SUMMARY: A greedy hyena's mean tricks on Monkey-Monkey eventually backfire when his victim finds out how he is being deceived.
[1. Monkeys—Fiction. 2. Hyenas—Fiction] I. Meisel, Paul, ill. II. Title. III. Series: Step into reading. Step 2 book.
PZ7.M478693Mo 1988 [E] 88-3072 ISBN: 0-394-89173-2 (pbk.); 0-394-99173-7 (lib. bdg.)

The rainy season was coming.

Monkey-Monkey had to build

a new house.

"Who will help me?" he asked.

"I would like to help,"
said Lion Mother.
"But I must go hunting.
My cubs are hungry."

"I would like to help,"

said Elephant Leader.

"But I must find

a new water hole for the herd."

"I would like to help,"
said Old Giraffe.
"But I hurt my hoof,
and it is hard to walk."

"Then I must build my house alone,"
said Monkey-Monkey.
And that is what he did.

"Dee diddle dee dum!"

Monkey-Monkey heard someone singing.

Hyena jumped out of the bushes.

"I see you are building a new house,"

he said.

"I will help you."

But Hyena was full of tricks.

Monkey-Monkey did not trust him.

"I will build my house alone,"

Monkey-Monkey told Hyena.

Hyena said, "Fine with me."

But before he left,

Hyena stole a banana.

Chomp! Chomp! Chomp!

He ate it all up.

"Stop eating my bananas!"

shouted Monkey-Monkey.

"And get going! Right now!"

"Hee hee ho!" Hyena laughed.

"That banana was so good!"

Then Hyena danced away.

Monkey-Monkey worked

on his house all day.

He did not get very far.

That night a Beautiful Creature
came out of the bushes.

The Beautiful Creature was singing.
"Dee diddle dee dum!"

"I know someone who sings that way,"
thought Monkey-Monkey.

"But who?"

14

The Beautiful Creature looked
at Monkey-Monkey's house.
"You need help," he said.
"I will help you.

But first you must make
a big pot of stew for me."

Monkey-Monkey did need help.
"Very well," he said.
"I will do as you ask.

Come back tomorrow."

Early the next morning

Monkey-Monkey made a big pot of stew.

Then all at once

an Ugly Monster jumped out

of the bushes.

Monkey-Monkey was afraid.

He ran up a tree.

He watched the Ugly Monster

eat up all the stew.

Chomp! Chomp! Chomp!

"I know someone who eats that way,"

thought Monkey-Monkey.

"But who?"

Then the Ugly Monster

ran back into the bushes.

A little later

the Beautiful Creature came back.

He looked in the empty pot.

"Where is my stew?" he asked.

Monkey-Monkey told him

about the Ugly Monster.

"That is too bad,"

said the Beautiful Creature.

"But I did not eat.

So I will not work for you."

"Please," said Monkey-Monkey.

"Come back tomorrow.

I will make another pot of stew."

The Beautiful Creature said that was fine.

Then he danced away.

"I know someone who dances that way,"

thought Monkey-Monkey.

"But who?"

19

Monkey-Monkey kept his word.

The next day

he made another big pot of stew.

All at once Monkey-Monkey heard

a noise in the bushes.

Was it the Beautiful Creature?

NO!

It was the Ugly Monster again!

Monkey-Monkey hid behind a log.

The Ugly Monster ate all the stew.

"Hee hee ho!" he laughed

as he ran away.

"I know someone who laughs that way,"

thought Monkey-Monkey.

"But who?"

Soon the Beautiful Creature came back.

Once again he looked in the pot.

"Too bad,"

said the Beautiful Creature.

"If I don't eat, I don't work.

But I will come back again tomorrow."

That's when Monkey-Monkey saw

a bit of stew

on the Beautiful Creature's face.

"Now, how did that get there?"

Monkey-Monkey said to himself.

Then he knew!

This time
Monkey-Monkey followed
the Beautiful Creature
down to the river.

The Beautiful Creature looked around.
Then he took off
his feathers.
It was Hyena!

Monkey-Monkey waited all night.

The next morning he saw

Hyena put mud and leaves

all over himself.

So Hyena was the Ugly Monster, too!

"I am so tricky!"

Hyena said, laughing.

"Hee hee ho!

I cannot wait to trick

Monkey-Monkey again."

"That is what he thinks!"

Monkey-Monkey said to himself.

Then he ran off

before Hyena saw him.

When the Ugly Monster
jumped out of the bushes,
another pot of stew
was bubbling and boiling.
But Monkey-Monkey was not there.
A very skinny Zebra
was stirring the pot of stew.

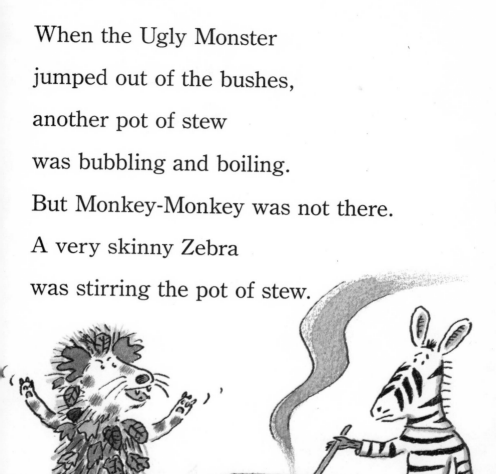

"Boo! Go away!"

shouted the Ugly Monster.

"Go away yourself!"

Zebra shouted back.

"You can't fool me.

You are not an Ugly Monster.

You are Hyena!"

The Ugly Monster took off

the leaves and mud.

"You are right!

Hee hee ho!"

Hyena laughed.

"I did not fool you.

But I did fool Monkey-Monkey."

Hyena smelled the big pot of stew.

"Where is Monkey-Monkey anyway?"

Zebra looked at him and said,

"He went to get more branches

for his house.

And if Monkey-Monkey finds out

about your trick,

he will be mad.

He will put a magic spell on you."

Hyena sat down.

He looked a little scared.

Zebra said,

"I used to be big and strong.

But I tricked Monkey-Monkey.

He found out

and put a spell on me.

Now look! I am so skinny."

Hyena jumped up.

He was really scared.

"Oh, no!" Hyena cried.

"How can I save myself?"

The skinny Zebra stirred the stew.
"You promised to help Monkey-Monkey
build his new house.
Maybe if you do,
he will not get too mad."

Hyena wasted no time.

He gathered branches and sticks.

He made lots of mud bricks.

Hyena worked all day
in the hot sun.
Zebra sat and watched.

At last

the house was finished.

"I hear Monkey-Monkey coming!"

shouted Zebra.

Hyena ran into the bushes.

"Tell Monkey-Monkey

I have gone away forever!"

he cried.

As soon as Hyena was gone,
Monkey-Monkey took off
the zebra skin.
"What a nice new house I have,"
he said happily.

Monkey-Monkey had a party
for his jungle friends.
He told them how
he had tricked Hyena.
All the animals laughed.

Then everybody sat down
and ate the big pot of stew!